DORLING KINDERSLEY *CLASSICS*

BLACK BEAUTY

Dorling Kindersley
LONDON, NEW YORK, SYDNEY, DELHI,
PARIS, MUNICH and JOHANNESBURG

ABRIDGED FOR YOUNG READERS

Art Editor Sarah Stanley
Senior Editor Marie Greenwood
Series Art Editor Jane Thomas
Research Fergus Day
Production Katy Holmes, Louise Barratt
Managing Art Editor Chris Fraser
Picture Research Louise Thomas and Elizabeth Bacon
DTP Designer Kim Browne
Abridgment Caryn Jenner

Published in the United States by Dorling Kindersley Publishing, Inc.
375 Hudson Street, New York, New York 10014

First American Edition, 1997
Paperback edition published in 2000
8 10 9 7

ISBN: 0-7566-1274-8

Color reproduction by Bright Arts
Printed and bound in China by L.Rex

For our complete
catalog visit
www.dk.com

DORLING KINDERSLEY CLASSICS

BLACK BEAUTY

ANNA SEWELL

Illustrated by
VICTOR AMBRUS

A Dorling Kindersley Book

CONTENTS

Black Beauty

Ginger

Merrylegs

James the stableboy

John Manly

Joe Green

Reuben Smith

Alfred Smirk

Jerry Barker

Captain

Nicholas Skinner

Introduction

When *Black Beauty* was first published in 1877 the title page read: *Black Beauty, his grooms and companions; the autobiography of a horse, translated from the original equine, by Anna Sewell.* Pretending that she had only translated a horse's own story from the "equine" gave Anna the freedom to write convincingly from the horse's point of view about what it was like to be entirely dependent on humans, whether they were kind or cruel.

Today we have cars and buses that don't need horses to pull them. Today if we need to contact a doctor we use the telephone instead of sending a horse and rider. So perhaps there aren't as many opportunities to be cruel to horses now that we don't rely on them as much. Times have changed.

It is easier to understand Black Beauty's times, when horses were treated like machines, if we can see the real carts and cabs, the buses and trams that they pulled – not just in an artist's impression, but in photographs of the real things.

It is also interesting to think about the characters in this book as real animals – they are born, grow, and develop exactly as horses do today. Again, it is easier to do this when we see photographs of real horses growing, being groomed, and revealing their highly developed senses.

Showing what made the times different – and how horses are still the same – is the special quality of the *Eyewitness Classic* edition of Anna Sewell's great translation "from the original equine."

Chapter one

MY FIRST HOME

GROWING UP
A newborn foal grows up quickly. Within an hour after birth it can stand up and begin to feed from its mother's milk.

When first born, a foal's legs wobble as it tries to stand up.

At two weeks, a foal has gained strength from its mother's milk.

At eight weeks, a foal eats grass, but still feeds from its mother's milk.

At four months, a foal sheds its milk hairs and grows an adult coat. Its legs are strong and sturdy.

At some time between five and six months, a foal is weaned. It stops taking milk from its mother and feeds by itself.

T HE FIRST PLACE that I can well remember was a large, pleasant meadow. Over the hedge on one side we looked into a plowed field, and on the other, the gate to our master's house. At the top of the meadow was a plantation of fir trees, and at the bottom a running brook overhung by a steep bank.

Our master was a good, kind man. He gave us good food, good lodgings, and kind words.

While I was young, I lived on my mother's milk, as I could not eat grass. In the daytime I ran by her side, and at night I lay down close by her. As soon as I was old enough to eat grass, my mother used to go out to work in the day and come back in the evening.

The other colts in the meadow were older than I was, some nearly as large as grown-up horses. I used to run with them and had great fun. We used to gallop all together round and round the field, as hard as we could go. Sometimes we had rather rough play, for the other colts would bite and kick as well as gallop.

One day, when there was a good deal of kicking, my mother whinnied to me to come to her, and then she said:

"You are well bred and well born. Your father has a great name in these parts, and your grandfather won the cup at the Newmarket races. Your grandmother had the sweetest temper of any horse I ever

knew, and I don't think you have ever seen me kick or bite. I hope
you will grow up gentle and good, never learn bad ways, and do
your work with a good will. Lift your feet up well when you trot,
and never bite or kick, even in play."

I have never forgotten my mother's advice; I knew she was a
wise old horse, and our master thought a great
deal of her. Her name was Duchess, but he
often called her Pet.

Newmarket
*"Your grandfather won the
cup at the Newmarket races."
Newmarket has been the very
center of British horse racing
for hundreds of years. A
winning racehorse was
bound to be well bred.*

*We used to gallop
all together round and
round the field, as hard
as we could go.*

HUNTING
Hunting was popular among wealthy people, and foxes or hares were the usual prey. Although many people are opposed to it because of its cruelty, the sport is still practiced today.

I was two years old when a circumstance happened which I have never forgotten. I and the other colts were feeding at the lower part of the field when we heard in the distance what sounded like the cry of dogs. The oldest of the colts raised his head, pricked his ears, and said, "There are the hounds!" and cantered off followed by the rest of us to the upper part of the field. My mother seemed to know all about it.

A hare wild with fright rushed by. On came the dogs, they burst over the bank, leaped across the stream, and came dashing

A hare wild with fright rushed by.

across the field, followed by the huntsmen. Six or eight men leaped their horses clean over, close upon the dogs. The hare tried to get through the fence, but it was too late. The dogs were upon her with their wild cries. Two fine horses were down, one was struggling in the stream, and the other was groaning on the grass. One of the riders was getting out of the water covered with mud, the other lay quite still.

"His neck is broken," said my mother.

My master was the first to reach the young man. He and the other riders carried him up to our master's house. I heard afterwards that it was George Gordon, the Squire's only son, and the pride of his family.

One of the horse's legs was broken.

Hunting kit
Traditionally, red jackets with white breeches are worn by huntsmen, while women wear black jackets with tan breeches.

Hunting cap

White breeches

Mahogany top boots are worn with a red coat.

Spurs

Hunting jacket

Hunting whip

Hunting horn

Hunting dogs
Dogs with a strong sense of smell are ideal for hunting. While foxhounds chase foxes, harriers are used for hunting hares. They are like foxhounds, but smaller.

Someone ran to our master's house and came back with a gun. Presently there was a loud bang and a dreadful shriek, and then all was still; the black horse moved no more. My mother seemed much troubled. She said that the horse's name was Rob Roy; he was a good, bold horse, and there was no vice in him. She never would go to that part of the field afterwards. I learned later that Rob Roy was Duchess's son, my older brother. It seems that horses have no relations: at least, they never know each other after they are sold.

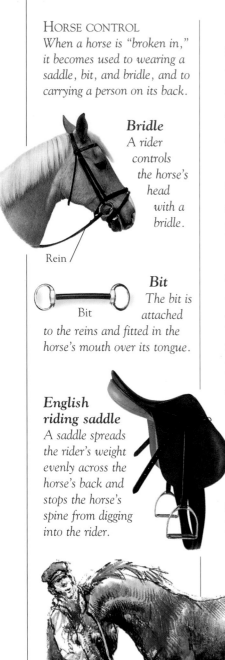

HORSE CONTROL
When a horse is "broken in,"
it becomes used to wearing a
saddle, bit, and bridle, and to
carrying a person on its back.

Bridle
A rider
controls
the horse's
head
with a
bridle.

Rein

Bit
The bit is
attached
Bit
to the reins and fitted in the
horse's mouth over its tongue.

English
riding saddle
A saddle spreads
the rider's weight
evenly across the
horse's back and
stops the horse's
spine from digging
into the rider.

I was now beginning to grow handsome; my coat had grown fine and soft, and was bright black. I had one white foot, and a pretty white star on my forehead. I was thought very handsome. My master would not sell me till I was four years old. He said lads ought not to work like men, and colts ought not to work like horses till they were quite grown up.

When I was four years old, Squire Gordon came to look at me. He examined my eyes, my mouth, and my legs. Then I had to walk, trot, and gallop before him. He seemed to like me, and said, "When he has been broken in, he will do very well."

Everyone may not know what breaking in is; therefore I will describe it. It means to teach a horse to wear a saddle and bridle and to carry on his back a man, woman, or child. Besides this he has to learn to wear a collar, then to have a cart fixed behind him. He must never start at what he sees, nor speak to other horses, nor bite, nor kick, nor have any will of his own, but always do his master's will, even though he may be tired or hungry. When the harness is on, he may neither jump for joy nor lie down for weariness.

I had long been used to a halter and to be led about in the fields and lanes, but now I was to have a bit and bridle. My master gave me some oats, and after a good deal of coaxing, he got the bit into my mouth, but it was a nasty thing! A piece of cold hard steel pushed into your mouth, with the ends held fast by straps. Next came the saddle. My master put it on my back gently, patting and talking to me all the time.

One morning, my master got on my back and rode me round the meadow. It did feel queer, but I felt proud to carry my master.

The next unpleasant business was putting on the iron shoes. My feet felt very stiff and heavy, but in time I got used to it.

As part of my training, my master

The next unpleasant business was
putting on the iron shoes.

12

sent me to a neighboring farm, which was skirted on one side by a railway.

I shall never forget the first train that ran by. I heard a strange sound at a distance, and with a rush and a clatter and a puffing of smoke a long black train of something flew by, and was gone almost before I could draw breath.

For the first few days I could not feed in peace, but as I found that this terrible creature never did me any harm, I began to disregard it.

My master often drove me in double harness with my mother. She told me the better I behaved, the better I should be treated. "There are many kinds of men," said she. "There are good, thoughtful men like our master, but there are cruel men, who never ought to have a horse to call their own. I hope you will fall into good hands, but a horse never knows who may buy him."

Age of steam
Early trains were pulled by horses, but horses were replaced gradually by steam engines, which were much more powerful. By the time Black Beauty was written, "iron horses" were a familiar sight, and vast railroad systems stretched across Europe and North America.

My master often drove me in double harness with my mother.

First, the horse's face is cleaned with a soft, damp cloth.

A coarse brush is used to remove any mud and surface dirt.

A softer body brush is then used to clean and massage the horse.

The groom removes any tail knots with his hand and then gently brushes the tail with a soft brush.

Chapter two

BIRTWICK PARK

I T WAS EARLY in May when there came a man from Squire Gordon's who took me away to Birtwick Park. My master said, "Good-bye. Be a good horse and always do your best." I put my nose into his hand. He patted me kindly, and I left my first home.

Squire Gordon's Park skirted the village of Birtwick. There was accommodation for many horses and carriages. In the stall next to mine stood a little, fat gray pony, with a thick mane and tail, a very pretty head, and a pert, little nose. This was Merrylegs.

A horse's head looked over at me from the stall beyond. The ears were laid back, and the eye looked rather ill-tempered. This was Ginger, a tall chestnut mare, with a long, handsome neck. She wanted to know about my upbringing and breaking in.

"If I had had your upbringing I might have as good a temper as you," said she. "My old master gave up the trade to his son, who had a hard voice and a hard hand. I felt that he wanted to wear all the spirit out of me. But John Manly says, 'Try her with kindness.' I have never snapped at him, and I won't either."

John Manly was the coachman. The next morning he gave me a good grooming, so that my coat was soft and bright. He rode me first slowly, then we went into a trot, then a canter, and when we were on the common we had a splendid gallop.

On our way back, we met the Squire and Mrs. Gordon walking. "Well, John, how does he go?"

"First-rate, sir," answered John. "He is as fleet as a deer and has a fine spirit, too, but the lightest touch of the rein will guide him."

The next day, I was brought up for my master. I remembered my mother's counsel, and I tried to do exactly what he wanted. I found that he was a good rider, and thoughtful for his horse, too. When we came home, the lady was at the door as he rode up.

"Well, my dear," she said, "how do you like him?"

"A pleasanter creature I never wished to mount," replied the Squire. "What shall we call him?"

"He is quite a beauty," said the lady. "Such a sweet face and a fine, intelligent eye. What do you say to calling him Black Beauty?"

I was quite happy in my new place. John talked to me a great deal. He seemed to know just how a horse feels, and when he cleaned me, he knew the tender places and the ticklish places. I went out with Ginger in the carriage, and we grew quite friendly, which made me feel very much at home.

What more could I want? Liberty! Now I was grown, I must stand up in a stable night and day except when I was wanted, and then be steady and quiet. It was a great treat for us to be turned out into the old orchard. The grass was so cool and soft to our feet, the air so sweet, and the freedom to do as we liked so pleasant. It was a very good time for talking, as we stood together under the shade of a large chestnut tree.

Hay rack

Grooming equipment

Victorian horse stall
Stables were divided into separate stalls. The horses were kept tied up and had no room to walk around, so they had to be taken out and exercised every day.

In the stall next to mine stood a little, fat gray pony, with a thick mane and tail.

High wheels meant that the cart moved quickly.

Dogcart
These light carriages were very popular. They were originally designed to take dogs to hunts or races. The dogs lay underneath the back seat.

The moment my feet touched the bridge, I felt sure there was something wrong.

One day in autumn, my master had to go on business, and John was to go with him. I was put into the dogcart, which is light, and runs along pleasantly on high wheels. There had been a great deal of rain, and now the wind was very high and blew the dry leaves across the road in a shower. We went along merrily till we came to a tollgate and a low wooden bridge. The man at the gate said the river was rising fast, and he feared it would be a bad night.

We got to the town, but as the master's business engaged him for a long time, we did not start for home till late in the afternoon. The wind was then much higher. Along the skirts of a wood, the great branches swayed about like twigs. Suddenly, there was a groan and a crack, and an oak came crashing down, and it fell right across the road before us. I trembled, but did not turn round or run away.

"That was a very near touch," said my master.

It was nearly dark.

We were going along at a good pace, but the moment my feet touched the bridge, I felt sure there was something wrong. I dared not go forward, and made a dead stop.

"Go on, Beauty," said my master, but I did not stir.

"There's something wrong, sir," said John, and he sprang out of the dogcart and tried to lead me. "Come, Beauty, what's the matter?"

Of course, I could not tell him, but I knew very well that the bridge was not safe.

Just then, the man at the tollgate ran out. "Stop!" he cried. "The bridge is broken in the middle and part of it is carried away. If you come on, you'll be into the river."

"You Beauty!" said John, and took the bridle and gently turned me round to the road.

For a good while, neither master nor John spoke, and then master began in a serious voice.

He said that God had given men reason, by which they could find out things for themselves, but He had given animals knowledge which did not depend on reason, and which was much more prompt and perfect in its way.

HORSE SENSE
Because horses have highly developed senses, they often show an uncanny ability to foretell danger.

Rearing
When horses rear, it is usually a sign that something is wrong. Horses also rear in play, or to show dominance.

Hearing
Horses have excellent hearing. Horses' ears move in the direction of a sound.

Listening to sounds behind

Listening to sounds from both directions

Listening to sounds in front

Touch
A horse has an acute sense of touch. A horse can feel a fly landing on its back and will whisk it away with its tail.

A PLACE TO REST
Coaching inns provided both travelers and their horses with refreshment, shelter from bad weather, and a comfortable bed for the night.

A typical inn sign

Guests arriving at an inn

Room at the inn

Large coaching inns were the best hotels in town, and a center for social life. Local people worked as maids, cooks, waiters, and grooms. Balls and card parties were held in assembly rooms.

Galleried guest bedrooms

Stables

Cobbled inner yard

A high arch allowed room for tall coaches.

Men gathered in the taprooms to drink.

Chapter three

AT THE INN

ONE MORNING IN EARLY DECEMBER, the master received a letter from his brother-in-law. He wanted the Squire to find him a trustworthy young groom.

"A steadier, pleasanter, honester, smarter young fellow than James, I never had in this stable," said John Manly. "Though he has not had much experience in driving, he has a light firm hand and quick eye, and he is very careful."

After this, it was decided by my master and mistress to pay a visit to some friends who lived some two days' ride away. James was to drive them, with Ginger and I pulling the carriage.

The first day, there were some long hills, but James drove carefully and kept our feet on the smoothest part of the road.

Just as the sun was going down, we reached the town where we were to spend the night. We drove under an archway into a long yard behind the inn, at the further end of which were the stables and coach houses. Two ostlers came to take us out. The head ostler was a pleasant, active little man with a crooked leg.

I never saw a man unbuckle a harness as quickly as he did, and with a pat and a good word, he led me to a long stable with six or eight stalls in it. The other man brought Ginger.

I never was cleaned so lightly and quickly as by that little old man. When he had done, James stepped up and felt me over, as if he thought I could not be thoroughly done, but he found my coat as clean and smooth as silk.

"I thought I was quick," said James, "and our John quicker still, but you do beat all."

"Practice makes perfect," said the ostler. "'Twould be a pity if it didn't. Forty years' practice, and not perfect! Ha, ha!"

Later in the evening, a traveler's horse was brought in by the second ostler, and while he was cleaning him, a young man with a pipe in his mouth lounged in the stable to gossip.

"I say, Towler," said the ostler, "just run up the ladder into the loft and put some hay into this horse's rack, will you? Only lay down your pipe first."

"All right," said Towler, and went up through the trapdoor.

I heard him step across the floor overhead. James came in to look at us last thing, and then the door was locked.

I cannot say how long I slept, but I woke feeling uncomfortable. I got up, the air seemed all thick and choking. I heard Ginger coughing, and one of the other horses moved about restlessly. It was quite dark and I could see nothing, but the stable was very full of smoke and I hardly knew how to breathe.

The trapdoor had been left open. I listened and heard a soft rushing sort of noise, and a low crackling and snapping.

The ostler
An ostler was an inn servant who helped care for the horses. He would unharness the tired horses on their arrival, feed them, and rub them down.

The horses were now all awake; some were pulling at their halters, others were stamping.

I did not know what it was, but there was something in the sound so strange that it made me tremble all over. The horses were now all awake; some were pulling at their halters, others were stamping.

Blindfold

Horses may refuse to be led because they are frightened. If blindfolded, they will often go willingly.

At last I heard steps outside, and the ostler who had put up the traveler's horse burst into the stable with a lantern. He began to untie the horses and try to lead them out. He seemed so frightened himself that he frightened me still more. The horses would not stir. He tried us all by turns and then left the stable. No doubt we were very foolish, but danger seemed to be all round. Then I heard a cry of "Fire!" outside, and the old ostler quietly and quickly came in. He got one horse out, and went to another, but the flames were playing round the trapdoor, and the roaring overhead was dreadful. The next thing I heard was James's voice, quiet and cheery, as it always was. "Come, Beauty, we'll soon be out of this smother."

He tied his scarf lightly over my eyes, and led me out of the stable.

FIRE FIGHTING
Fire engines were pulled by dapple-gray horses, because they were easier to see through smoke or in the dark. This engine carried the ladders and other equipment.

Safe in the yard, he slipped the scarf off my eyes, and darted back inside. I set up a shrill whinny as I saw him go. Ginger told me afterward that was the best thing I could have done, for had she not heard me, she would never

"'Tis the fire engine! Make way!"

have had the courage to come out.

There was much confusion in the yard, but I kept my eye fixed on the stable door, where the smoke poured out thicker than ever. The next moment I gave a loud, joyful neigh, for I saw James coming through the smoke leading Ginger.

"My brave lad," said my master, "are you hurt?"

James shook his head, for he could not yet speak.

"'Tis the fire engine! Make way!" shouted two or three voices as two horses dashed into the yard with the heavy engine behind them. The firemen leaped to the ground. We got out as fast as we could into the broad, quiet marketplace. The stars were shining, and except for the noise behind us, all was still.

The next morning, James said that two poor horses that could not be got out were buried under the burned rafters and tiles.

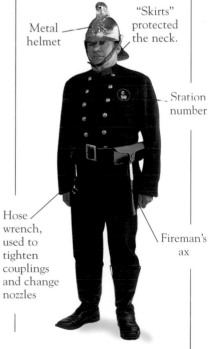

Firefighter

Four firefighters manned the engine. They were on duty for more than 100 hours a week.

"Skirts" protected the neck.

Metal helmet

Station number

Hose wrench, used to tighten couplings and change nozzles

Fireman's ax

Beauty sleep
Horses can sleep while standing up. They lock special joints in their legs to keep themselves upright.

Chapter four

THE NEW STABLEBOY

LITTLE JOE GREEN was to take James's place as stableboy. "Why he is a child!" said James.

"Fourteen and a half," said John Manly, "but he is quick, and willing, and kind-hearted, too. He wishes very much to come."

One night, a few days after James had left, I was suddenly awakened by the stable bell ringing loudly.

"Wake up, Beauty, you must go well now, if ever you did," said John Manly, and almost before I could think, he had got the saddle on my back and the bridle on my head.

"Ride for your life, John, that is, for your mistress's life," said the Squire. "Give this note to Dr. White. Then give your horse a rest at the inn, and be back as soon as you can."

John said, "Yes, sir," and was on my back in a minute.

I galloped as fast as I could lay my feet to the ground.

Horses can reach speeds of 40 mph (65 km/h)

Away we went through the Park. I wanted no whip nor spur; I galloped as fast as I could lay my feet to the ground; I don't believe that my old grandfather who won the race at Newmarket could have gone faster. The air was frosty, the moon was bright, it was very pleasant. We came through the village, then through a dark wood, then uphill, then downhill, till after an eight-mile run, we came to the town. It was all quite still, except the clatter of my feet upon the stones – everybody was asleep.

The church clock struck three as we drew up at Dr. White's door. John rang the bell twice, and then knocked at the door like thunder. A window was thrown open, and Dr. White, in his nightcap, put his head out and said, "What do you want?"

"Mrs. Gordon is very ill, sir; Master wants you to go at once."

"My horse has been out all day and is quite done up, and my son has taken the other," said the doctor. "Can I have your horse?"

"He has come at a gallop nearly all the way, sir, and I was to give him a rest here. But Black Beauty will go till he drops."

John stroked my neck. I was very hot. "Take care of Beauty, sir," he said. "I should not like any harm to come to him."

In a minute, we had left John far behind.

The doctor was a heavier man than John, and not so good a rider; however, I did my very best. When we came to a hill, the doctor drew me up. "Now, my good fellow," he said, "take some breath." I was glad he did, for I was nearly spent, but that breathing helped me on, and soon we were in the Park. Joe was at the lodge gate, my master was at the hall door, for he had heard us coming. The doctor went into the house with him, and Joe led me to the stable.

At a gallop
The gallop is a horse's fastest natural gait (pace), during which there is a time when all four feet are off of the ground.

Calves pressed close to horse

English riding position
English riders sit centrally in the saddle, keeping an upright and relaxed posture. The balls of the feet are kept on the stirrups.

Doctor's orders
Doctors often traveled on horseback. They needed horses that could cover long distances quickly in an emergency. Many doctors that owned only one horse walked to see their patients on Sunday to give their horse a rest.

He rubbed my legs and my chest, but he did not put my warm cloth on me.

Strap to secure blanket

Blanket fitted to shape of horse

Keeping warm
After heavy exercise, a horse needs to be kept warm. A thick blanket is fitted around the horse to prevent it from losing too much body heat. Gruel, made from oats and water, was often fed to the horse because it was easy to digest.

I was glad to get home. My legs shook under me, and I could only stand and pant. I had not a dry hair on my body, the water ran down my legs, and I steamed all over – Joe used to say like a pot on the fire. Poor Joe! As yet, he knew very little, but I am sure he did the very best he knew. He rubbed my legs and my chest, but he did not put my warm cloth on me; he thought I was so hot, I should not like it. Then he gave me a pail full of water to drink; it was cold and very good and, I drank it all. Then he gave me some hay and some corn, and thinking he had done right, he went away.

Soon I began to shake and tremble, and turned deadly cold. My legs ached, my loins ached, and my chest ached, and I felt sore all over. Oh! How I wished for my warm, thick cloth as I stood and trembled. I wished for John, but he had eight miles to walk, so I lay down in my straw and tried to go to sleep.

After a long while, I heard John at the door. I gave a low moan, for I was in great pain. He was at my side in a moment, stooping down by me. I could not tell him how I felt, but he seemed to know it all. He covered me up with warm cloths, and then ran to the house for some hot water. He made me some warm gruel, which I drank, and then I think I went to sleep.

I was very ill. A strong inflammation had attacked my lungs, and I could not draw my breath without pain. John nursed me night and day; my master, too, often came to see me.

"My poor Beauty," he said one day, "you saved your mistress's life!"

I was very glad to hear that. John told my master he never saw a horse go so fast in his life, it seemed as if the horse knew what was the matter. Of course I did, though John thought not. At least I knew as much as this, that John and I must go at top speed, and that it was for the sake of the mistress.

I do not know how long I was ill. Mr. Bond, the horse doctor, came every day. One day he bled me; John held a pail for the blood. I felt very faint after it, and thought I should die, and I believe they all thought so, too.

One night John had to give me a draft. Thomas Green came to help him, and said in a low voice:

"I wish, John, you'd say a bit of a kind word to Joe. The boy is quite heartbroken, he can't eat his meals, and he can't smile. He says he knows it was all his fault, though he is sure he did the best he knew. It goes to my heart to hear him."

"I know he meant no harm," said John slowly. "I never said he did. But you see, I am sore myself; that horse is the pride of my heart, and to think that his life may be flung away in this manner is more than I can bear. But if you think I am hard on the boy, I will try to give him a good word tomorrow – that is, if Beauty is better."

"Well, John, I knew you did not wish to be too hard, and I am glad you see it was only ignorance."

John's voice almost startled me as he answered.

"*Only* ignorance! Only *ignorance*! Don't you know that it is the worst thing in the world, next to wickedness? And which does the most mischief, heaven only knows."

I heard no more of this conversation, for the medicine did well and sent me to sleep, and in the morning I felt much better. But I often thought of John's words when I came to know more of the world.

I could not draw my breath without pain.

Treating horses
Horses were bled to help get rid of any infection. A small cut was made in a vein, usually in the horse's neck.

A rope was used to help raise the horse's head.

Giving a draft
A draft, or liquid medicine, was poured slowly into the horse's mouth.

Hollowed horn for giving medicine

25

Joe Green went on very well. He learned quickly, and John began to trust him in many things, though it was seldom that he was allowed to exercise either Ginger or me.

It so happened one morning that John was out, and the master wanted a note to be taken to a gentleman's house. He sent his orders for Joe to saddle me and take it.

The note was delivered, and we were quietly returning till we came to the brickfield. Here we saw a cart heavily laden with bricks. The wheels had stuck fast in the stiff mud, and the carter was shouting and flogging the two horses unmercifully.

Joe pulled up.

Bricklaying
Bricks were made in brickfields, in areas where clay could be found. Horses were used to pull heavy loads of bricks from the brickfield to the construction site.

"Hold hard," said Joe. "Don't go flogging the horses like that."

There were the two horses straining and struggling to drag the cart out, but they could not move it. The man swore and lashed most brutally.

"Hold hard," said Joe. "Don't go flogging the horses

like that. The wheels are so stuck that they cannot move the cart."
The man took no heed, but went on lashing.

"Pray, stop!" said Joe. "I'll help you to lighten your cart."

"Mind your own business, you impudent young rascal!"

The man laid on the whip again.

Joe turned my head, and the next moment we were going at a round gallop toward the house of the master brickmaker.

"There's a fellow flogging two horses to death. Pray, sir, go." Joe's voice shook with excitement.

The master brickmaker was soon gone, and we were on our way home at a smart trot.

Carts and carters
Horses had to pull all kinds of wagons and were often cruelly beaten by the carter if their pace slackened.

Later, the footman came to say that Joe was wanted in master's private room. There was a man brought up for ill-using horses, and Joe's evidence was wanted. Our master being one of the county magistrates, cases were often brought to him to settle.

When Joe next came into the stable, I saw he was in high spirits. He gave me a good-natured slap and said, "We won't see such things done, will we, old fellow?"

We heard afterwards that the carter was committed to trial, and might be sentenced to two or three months in prison.

It was wonderful what a change had come over Joe. He was just as kind and gentle as before, but there was more purpose and determination in all that he did – as if he had jumped at once from a boy to a man.

Bridle   Collar   Driving saddle   Breeching strap

Harnessed for work
Horses wear harnesses to help them pull wagons and carriages. A harness is made up of a bridle, collar, and breeching.

Illness
In the nineteenth century the cure for many illnesses was thought to be a change of climate. Some ailments were more difficult to cure.

Ponies have small, compact bodies.

Pony ride
Ponies are horses that are less than 58 inches (147 cm) high. Their small size and gentle nature make them ideal for children to ride.

Merrylegs he had given to the vicar.

Chapter five

THE PARTING

I HAD NOW LIVED IN THIS HAPPY PLACE for three years, but sad changes were about to come over us. We heard from time to time that our mistress was ill. The doctor was often at the house, and the master looked grave and anxious. Then we heard that she must leave her home and go to a warm country. The master began directly to make arrangements for leaving England.

John went about his work silent and sad, and Joe scarcely whistled. There was a great deal of coming and going.

The first of the party who went were Miss Jessie and Flora with their governess. They came to bid us good-bye. They hugged poor Merrylegs like an old friend, and so indeed he was.

Then we heard what had been arranged for us. Master had sold Ginger and me to his friend, the Earl, for he thought we should have a good place there. Merrylegs he had given to the vicar, who had a large family of boys and girls. Joe was engaged to take care of him, so I thought that Merrylegs was well off.

The evening before they left, the master came into the stable to give his horses a gentle pat. He seemed very low-spirited; I knew by his voice. I believe we horses can tell more by the voice than men can.

"Have you decided what to do, John?" he asked.

"I have made up my mind that if I could get a situation with some first-rate colt-breaker and horsetrainer, that it would be the right thing for me," said John. "Many young animals are frightened and spoiled by the wrong treatment. I always get on well with horses, and if I could help some of them to a fair start, I should feel as if I was doing some good."

"You understand horses, John," said the Squire, "and somehow they understand you."

The last sad day had come. Ginger and I brought the carriage up to the Hall door for the last time. Master came down the steps carrying the mistress in his arms. He placed her carefully in the carriage, while the house servants stood round crying.

"Goodbye, again. We shall not forget any of you," he said.

When we reached the railway station, Joe took the things out of the carriage. John called to him to stand by the horses, while he went on the platform. Poor Joe! He stood close up to our heads to hide his tears. Very soon the train came puffing into the station. Then the doors were slammed to, the guard whistled, and the train glided away, leaving behind it only clouds of white smoke, and some very heavy hearts.

When it was out of sight, John came back. He took the reins, mounted the box, and drove slowly home; but it was not our home now.

A good trainer
The best type of horsetrainer is, like John, patient and kind. The different elements of breaking in, such as fitting the bit and using the saddle, are introduced gradually.

Very soon the train came puffing into the station.

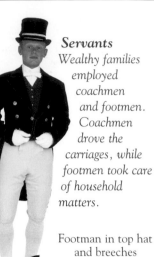

Servants
*Wealthy families
employed
coachmen
and footmen.
Coachmen
drove the
carriages, while
footmen took care
of household
matters.*

Footman in top hat
and breeches

Chapter six

EARLSHALL

JOHN PUT THE SADDLE ON GINGER and the leading rein on me, and rode us about fifteen miles to Earlshall Park. We were placed in boxes adjoining each other. Mr. York, who was to be our new coachman, came in to see us.

"The black one has a perfect temper. The chestnut came to us snappish, but if well-treated there is not a more willing animal. I had better mention, we never used the bearing rein with either of them."

"His Lordship is reasonable about horses," said York, "but my lady will have style. Her carriage horses must be reined up tight."

"I am sorry for it, very sorry," said John.

He came round to pat us for the last time. I held my face close to him.

Ginger reared up suddenly.

Then he was gone, and I have never seen him since.

In the afternoon we were put in the carriage and led round to the front of the house. Two footmen were standing ready, with scarlet breeches and white stockings. Presently we heard the rustling sound of silk as my lady came down the flight of stone steps. Though it certainly was a nuisance not to be able to get my head down now and then, the bearing rein did not pull my head higher than I was accustomed to carry it.

The next day, the lady said in an imperious voice, "York, you must put those horses' heads higher. They are not fit to be seen."

York shortened the rein one hole, but every little makes a difference. I wanted to put my head forward and take the carriage up the hill with a will. But I had to pull with my head up now, and that took the spirit out of me, and the strain came on my back and legs.

When we came in, Ginger said, "Now you see what it is like. If it does not get much worse, I shall say nothing, for we are well treated here. But if they strain me up tight, why, let 'em look out!"

Day by day our bearing reins were shortened. Instead of looking forward to having my harness put on, I began to dread it.

One day, my lady said, "Raise the bearing reins at once, York, and let us have no more of this humoring and nonsense."

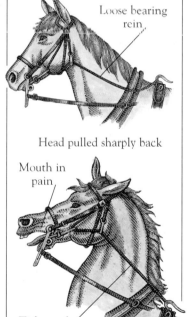

York fixed my rein so tight it was almost intolerable. Then he went to Ginger. The moment he took the rein off, she reared up so suddenly, that York had his hat knocked off. At last, she kicked right over the carriage pole and fell down. There is no knowing what further mischief she might have done, had not York promptly sat on her head to prevent her struggling.

"Confound these bearing reins!" he said to himself.

When Ginger was well of her bruises, one of the Lord's sons said he should like to have her for hunting. As for me, I was obliged still to go in the carriage.

A STYLISH BEARING
For the sake of fashion, discomfort was endured. Women of wealth and position pinched in their waists with corsets and made themselves ill. The horses that pulled their carriages also had to be stylish and uncomfortable.

Normal head position

Loose bearing rein

Head pulled sharply back

Mouth in pain

Tightened bearing rein

The bearing rein
Horses were made to wear a bearing rein, or checkrein. This short rein forced the horse to hold its head high and prevented it from standing in its usual position.

THE COUNTRY HORSE

The large country houses of Victorian England were home to some fine horses, like Black Beauty. After happy years at Birtwick Park, he moved to the even grander Earlshall, but found people were more concerned with style than horse care.

Country outings

Wealthy people like the Earl and his wife could afford their own carriages and would want the most elegant, light horses, like Black Beauty and Ginger, to drive them in style.

Grand hall

Big country houses, like Earlshall, were surrounded by outbuildings. Visitors would arrive at a grand entrance, and footmen would stand ready to gree them at the door.

Dairy

Garden

When the order was given, horses were harnessed and a carriage brought to the front of the house.

The coachman drove the carriages.

The sweeping drive enabled carriages to turn with ease.

WORKING IN THE COUNTRY

Horses were used in the countryside in agriculture, for transportation, and in forestry, as well as for leisure and sports, such as hunting.

Farming

Before farmers had tractors, strong, heavy horses were used for many farm tasks, such as pulling plows (below), rakes, and carts. Heavy horses were especially bred for this type of work.

Barge pulling

One to two horses (known as "boaters") were needed to pull heavy goods barges. Canals covered much of Britain, and transported coal, wood, and other cargo, as well as passengers.

WORKING IN THE STABLES

Coachman

In addition to being the carriage driver, the coachman was responsible for taking care of the horses and the stables. He was in charge of the grooms and the stableboys. York was the head coachman at Earlshall.

Horses would roam the orchard and eat apples that the wind had blown down.

Coachman's cottage

The coachman could get to the stable block very easily from here, and he could grow his own food in the small garden provided.

HORSE FODDER

Horses need a good mix of grain, fruit, and vegetables in their diet. The horses' food was kept in a separate storeroom. Dried food, such as oats, bran, and cornmeal, was kept in large bins. Some fresh vegetables and fruit were grown on the grounds of the estate.

Bran

Oats

WHERE HORSES LIVED

Light, well-ventilated, and well-drained stables were important for keeping horses healthy. Everything needed to care for the horses was in the stable block.

Hayrack   Loose ring   Manger for feeding

Stall

Blocks of stalls could house many horses in the stables, but the horse was tied to the wall that it faced, and could only stand up or lie down.

Loose box

This was a larger space enclosed by wooden sides with iron bars across the top. It gave the horse more freedom to move around, but it took up more space.

Horses were exercised in the paddock.

Large stable blocks were seen as a sign of wealth because they reflected the number of horses an estate had.

Food store

Clocktower

Barouche carriage

Loose box

Stall

Horses were groomed in the stableyard.

Coach house at the front of the stable block

Carriages were cleaned in the stableyard and were kept in the coach house.

The stableboy of the house

Tack room

Groom

The groom was in charge of feeding, grooming, and exercising the horses. At large houses like Arlshall, there would be more than one groom, each with a special job.

Stableboy

The stableboy cleaned out and swept the stable, cleaned and tidied the harnesses and other equipment, and helped the groom take care of the horses.

Stairs leading to staff quarters

Saddles and cleaning equipment

Harnesses and straps

Tackroom

This was where the saddles and other equipment were kept. It was heated, and the staff often lived in rooms above.

Rider sits on
left side.

Whip

Riding
gloves

RIDING SIDESADDLE
*The only way a woman
wearing long, heavy skirts
could sit comfortably on
a horse was by riding
sidesaddle. The rider
supported her leg by
bending it around a pommel.*

Pommel   Seat

Side-
saddle

Single
stirrup

In the spring, my Lord went to London, and took York with him.
I and some other horses were left at home. Lady Harriet, who
remained at the Hall, was a great invalid, and never went out in the
carriage, and the Lady Anne preferred riding on horseback.

There was a gentleman of the name of Blantyre staying at the
Hall who always rode Lizzie, a bay mare with a lively spirit.

One day Lady Anne ordered the sidesaddle to be put on
Lizzie, and the other saddle on me.

"Do let me advise you not to mount her," said Blantyre. "Lizzie is
a charming creature, but too nervous for a lady."

"Pray do not trouble your good head about me," said Lady Anne,
laughing, "and help me to mount, like the good friend you are."

Blantyre placed her carefully on Lizzie's saddle, then mounted me.
Just as we were moving off, a footman came with a message from the
Lady Harriet to be delivered to Dr. Ashley.

The doctor's house was
the last in the village.

*With one determined
leap I cleared both
dyke and bank.*

Blantyre alighted and hung my rein on the gate.

Lizzie stood quietly by the side of the road. My mistress was sitting easily with a loose rein, humming a little song.

Just then, some cart horses and young colts came trotting out of a meadow on the opposite side of the road, while a boy behind was cracking a great whip. One of the colts bolted across the road, and blundered up against Lizzie's hind legs. Whether it was the stupid colt or the loud cracking of the whip, or both together, I cannot say, but she gave a violent kick, and dashed off into a headlong gallop.

I gave a loud neigh for help, tossing my head to get the rein loose. Blantyre sprang into the saddle and we dashed after them.

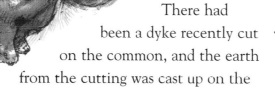

There had been a dyke recently cut on the common, and the earth from the cutting was cast up on the other side. With scarcely a pause, Lizzie took the leap, stumbled, and fell.

I gathered myself well together, and with one determined leap cleared both dyke and bank. Motionless among the heather, with her face to the earth, lay my poor young mistress.

Two men had seen Lizzie running wild without a rider.

"Mount this horse," Blantyre told the foremost man, "and ride to the doctor's, then on to the Hall. Bid them to send help."

The man scrambled into the saddle, and with a "Gee-up" and a clap on my sides, he did his errand like a good man and true. Two days after the accident, I found out that my young mistress was out of danger, and would soon be able to ride again. This was good news to me.

Helping hand
It was difficult to mount a horse when riding sidesaddle, and women were usually helped by a groom. He would lock his hands together to form a step, then hoist her up into the saddle.

Horses sometimes rear up before they bolt.

Taking flight
Horses are suspicious of anything strange, and when frightened by a sudden noise or movement, they may take flight, or bolt. Experienced riders always try to anticipate hazards.

It is difficult for a rider to stop a bolting horse.

Brougham

These light, enclosed carriages carried two people. They were drawn by one horse and were used in towns.

Driver's seat

Surgical shoe for horses with foot problems

Nails

Ordinary shoe

Horseshoes

When a horse is ridden on rough ground, its hooves may break. Iron horseshoes are fitted to protect them. They are custom-made for each horse.

Pincers for pulling out old nails

Nailing a shoe

Farrier

A farrier was a horse doctor as well as someone who fitted horseshoes. The method of shoeing horses has not changed since Black Beauty's time.

I must now say a little about Reuben Smith, who was left in charge when York went to London. When he was all right, there could not be a more valuable man. He was gentle and very clever with horses, and could doctor them as well as a farrier. But Smith had one great fault, and that was the love of drink. He had promised never to taste another drop, and had kept this promise so well that York thought he might now be trusted.

But Smith had one fault, and that was drink.

It was April, and the family was expected home in May. The brougham was to be freshly done up, and it was arranged that Smith should leave the carriage at the maker's and ride back, and I was chosen for the journey.

We left the carriage at the maker's, and Smith rode me to the *White Lion* and ordered the ostler to have me ready at four o'clock. Smith did not come into the yard till five, and said he should not leave till six, as he had met with some old friends. The ostler told him of a loose nail in one of my front shoes.

"That will be all right till we get home," said Smith in an offhand way. I thought it was unlike him not to see about loose nails.

It was nearly nine before he called for me, and he seemed in a very bad temper. Almost before he was out of the town he began to gallop, frequently giving me a sharp cut with his whip, though I was going at full speed. The roads were stony, and going over them at this pace my shoe became looser until it came off. But Smith was too madly drunk to notice anything.

My shoeless foot suffered dreadfully. The hoof was split and the inside cut. This could not go on. I stumbled and fell with violence on both my knees. Smith was flung off by my fall. There was a heavy groan, but I could see no motion. Nothing moved but the white clouds near the moon.

It must have been nearly midnight when I heard the sound of a horse's feet. I hoped it might be someone coming in search of us. I neighed, and was overjoyed to hear a neigh from Ginger, and men's voices. They stopped at the figure on the ground.

One of the men stooped over it. "It is Reuben! He is dead."

They raised him up, but there was no life. They laid him down and came and looked at me. They soon saw my cut knees.

"Why, the horse has thrown him!" said the other.

Robert the groom attempted to lead me, but I almost fell again.

"Look here. He's bad in his foot as well as his knees. Ned, I'm afraid it hasn't been all right with Reuben. Just think of him riding a horse over these stones without a shoe!"

It was agreed that Robert should lead me, and Ned must take the body in the dogcart. Robert bound his handkerchief round my foot, and so led me home.

Treating a horse
A horse's feet and knees are vulnerable to injury. Wounds are cleaned before being dressed and bandaged.

Knee injury
If a leg is bandaged at once, it will help the knee heal quickly.

I stumbled and fell with violence on both my knees. Smith was flung off by my fall.

There were the tight-rein drivers …

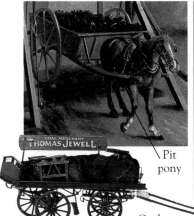

Then there were loose-rein drivers. These were often careless altogether.

Pit pony

Coal cart

Coal carting
Horses traveled long distances pulling heavy loads of coal from railroad stations to villages and farms in remote areas. Ponies were used to haul coal out of the mines, or pits.

As soon as my knees were sufficiently healed, I was turned into a small meadow. One morning the gate opened, and who should come in but dear old Ginger. She had been ruined by hard riding, and was now turned off to rest.

"Here we are," she said, "ruined in the prime of our youth."

About a week after this, I was bought by the master of a livery stables. Ginger and I neighed to each other as I was led off.

In the livery stables I was to get experience of different kinds of bad driving. I was now a "job-horse," let out to people who wished to hire me. There were the tight-rein drivers, who thought that all depended on holding the reins as hard as they could. Then there were loose-rein drivers, who let the reins lie easily on our backs, and had no control. These drivers were often careless altogether. I went out in the phaeton one day. My driver was laughing and joking with the lady and children, but he never thought to keep an eye on his horse, and I soon got a stone in one of my forefeet.

He chucked the reins and flipped about with the whip, saying, "They have sent us out with a lame horse!"

A farmer came riding up. He drew a stonepick out of his pocket. Very carefully, as the stone was tightly wedged, he got it out.

This was the sort of experience we job-horses often came in for.

I well remember one spring evening Rory and I had been out for the day. (Rory went with me when a pair was ordered, and a good fellow he was.) We were coming home at a smart pace. Our road turned to the left. We were close to the hedge on our own side and there was room to pass. As we neared the corner, I heard a horse and two wheels coming rapidly down the hill toward us. The man who was driving made straight for the corner. When he came in sight of us, he was going so fast, he had no time to pull over to his own side.

Happily for me, I was on the side next to the hedge. The whole shock came upon Rory. The gig shaft ran right into his chest, making him stagger back with a cry I shall never forget.

The driver was one of those ignorant fellows who don't know which is their own side of the road, or if they know, don't care.

It was a long time before Rory's wound healed, and then he was sold for coal carting – and what that is, only horses know.

HORSE FOR HIRE

HIRING COSTS

It cost 16 shillings (about $1.60) to hire a horse, carriage, and one driver for the day, about the same as a stableboy's weekly wage. Drivers – hired by the hour, the day, or for longer periods – earned up to 30 shillings (about $3.00) a week.

W hen Black Beauty was sold to a livery stable he joined a variety of horses – from the heavy cart horse to the little pony – who were rented out to do many different jobs. Horses were rented complete with a harness and carriage.

This light horse has an upright neck and powerful shoulders, making it an ideal carriage horse.

Traveling in style
Horses were often hired out in well-matched pairs that kept in stride. These gray horses are pulling an open-topped phaeton.

Barouche
This open carriage was built to a French design, and was often hired out by couples going for summer outings in the park and country.

Seating for two

Gig
The light, two-wheeled gig was popular with young gentlemen. It was easy to drive, inexpensive to run, and needed only one horse.

Livery stable
Both horses and carriages for rent were kept in livery stables. Eight or nine horses were kept in one stable.

Job masters were in charge of the livery stables.

The horse was harnessed between long shafts.

Heavy horses
Heavy horses are broadly built, powerful animals. Some of the larger breeds weighed up to 2,200 lb (1,000 kg).

Heavy horses have short backs and legs and broad chests.

Drays are low, flat carts.

Pulling power
Heavy horses were rented by tradespeople to pull wagons, barges, and brewers' drays, or by farmers to pull plows.

Alfred Smirk considered himself very handsome.

Chapter seven

SOLD AGAIN

OF COURSE, WE SOMETIMES CAME IN for good driving. One gentleman took a great liking to me, and prevailed upon my master to sell me to a friend of his who wanted a safe, pleasant horse for riding.

My new master lived in Bath, and was engaged in business. He knew little about horses, but treated me well, and I should have had a good place but for circumstances of which he was ignorant.

If ever there was a humbug in the shape of a groom, Alfred Smirk was the man. He considered himself very handsome, and spent a great deal of time about his hair, whiskers, and necktie before a little looking glass in the harness room.

He was very civil to me. In fact, he did a great deal of stroking and patting, when his master was there to see it.

He always brushed my mane and tail with water to make me look smart. But as to cleaning my feet, or grooming me thoroughly, he thought no more of that than if I had been a cow. I had a loose box, and might have been very comfortable if he had not been too indolent to clean it out. He never took all the straw away, and the smell from what lay underneath was very bad. It made my eyes smart, and I did not feel the same appetite for my food.

One day, his master came in and said, "Alfred, the stable smells rather strong. Should you not give that stall a good scrub, and throw down plenty of water?"

"I'll do so if you please, sir," said Alfred, touching his cap, "but it is rather dangerous, sir, throwing down water in a horse's box, they are very apt to take cold, sir."

"Well," said the master, "do you think the drains are all right?"

The bricklayer came and pulled up a great many bricks, and found nothing amiss. The smell in my box was as bad as ever.

Standing as I did on moist straw, my feet grew unhealthy and tender, and the master used to say: "I don't know what is the matter with this horse, he goes very fumble-footed."

MUCKING OUT
Old bedding, droppings, and urine can quickly make a stable smell. Stables should be cleaned out every day.

Cleaning the hooves
If a horse is kept in a dirty stable, its hooves can become tender and infected. Hooves and heels should be washed regularly.

"Yes, sir," said Alfred, "I have noticed the same myself, when I have exercised him."

Now the fact was he hardly ever did exercise me, and when the master was busy, I often stood for days without stretching my legs.

One day my feet were so tender, I made two such serious stumbles that he stopped at the farrier's to see what was the matter with me. The man took up my feet one by one and examined them.

"This is the sort of thing we find in foul stables," he said.

The next day I had my feet thoroughly cleansed and soaked in some strong lotion. The farrier ordered all the litter to be taken out of my box day by day, and the floor kept very clean.

With this treatment, I soon regained my spirits, but my master was so disgusted at being deceived by his groom that he determined to give up keeping a horse. I was therefore kept until my feet were quite sound, and then sold again.

Warming up
A stabled horse needs exercise every day. Before riding it should be warmed up by walking and trotting for about 20 minutes.

"Alfred, the stable smells rather strong."

41

I knew by the way he handled me that he was used to horses.

Bright, alert eyes

Smooth, shiny coat

Even, strong feet

What they looked for
Buyers examined a horse for signs of neglect and disease. They also checked that its proportions were well balanced. In Britain people pay with currency called pounds.

No doubt a horse fair is a very amusing place to those who have nothing to lose, but if a horse may speak his mind so far as he understands, there were more lies told, and more trickery at that horse fair, than a clever man could give account of. The gentlemen always turned from me when they saw my broken knees; though the man who had me swore it was only a slip in the stall.

The first thing was to pull my mouth open, then to look at my eyes, then feel all the way down my legs, and give me a hard feel of the skin and flesh, and then try my paces. It was wonderful what a difference there was in the way these things were done. Some did it in a rough, offhand way, as if one was only a piece of wood; while others would take their hands gently over one's body, with a pat now and then, as much as to say, "by your leave." Of course I judged a good deal of the buyers by their manners to myself.

There was one man, I thought, if he would buy me, I should be happy. I knew in a moment, by the way he handled me, that he was used to horses; he spoke gently, and his gray eyes had a kindly, cheery look in them. He offered twenty-three pounds for me; but that was refused, and he walked away. I looked after him, but he was gone, and a very hard-looking, loud-voiced man came and offered twenty-three pounds. A very close bargain was being driven; for my salesman began to think he should not get all he asked, and must come down; but just then the gray-eyed man came back again. I could not help reaching out my head towards him. He stroked my face kindly.

"Well, old chap," he said, "I think we should suit each other. I'll give twenty-four for him."

"Say twenty-five and you shall have him."

"Twenty-four ten," said my friend, "and not another sixpence."

"Done," said the salesman.

The money was paid on the spot, and my new master led me out of the fair to an inn, where he gave me a good feed of oats. He stood by while I ate it, talking to me. Half an hour after, we were on our way to London, through pleasant lanes and country roads, until we came into the great London thoroughfare, on which we traveled steadily, till in the twilight we reached the great city.

At the Fair

Horse fairs were noisy, lively places, with lots of arguing, bidding, and money changing hands. Many different types of horses were paraded in front of buyers from all walks of life, from the wealthy landowner to the lowly cabdriver. Black Beauty was now worth less because of his broken knees, but fortunately he was bought by the gentle and kind Jerry Barker.

Buyer checking the horse's teeth

How to tell a horse's age

The buyer could tell a horse's age by checking its teeth. From about 12 years of age, the front teeth slope outward and the gums shrink, making the teeth seem longer. This becomes more obvious with age.

Horses for courses

Buyers looked for different qualities in a horse, depending on their needs. Light horses, like Black Beauty, were always in demand for pulling carriages and cabs.

This palomino pony has a gold coat with white mane and tail.

Good-natured ponies were ideal for children learning to ride.

Chestnut coat

Buyers checking over horses

Horse fairs were social events to which people traveled from many miles around.

This light horse was ideal for carriage work, though chestnut horses, like Ginger, were said to have hot tempers

Graceful neck

Fine, tall thoroughbred racehorses were the most expensive breed.

Fine, silky coat

Wide, strong body

Fair deal

Buyers needed to be quite experienced with horses and know what to look for. Otherwise, traders would often try to cheat their customers. Wealthy buyers might employ professionals to check the horses for them.

In England, certain places were regular sites for horse fairs, such as this one in Barnet, north London.

Black beauty's value

Black Beauty and Ginger were in good condition when they were sold as a pair for $17,000 to the Earl. Jerry paid $1,390 for Black Beauty at the fair. Later, tired out from cabdriving, he was sold for $284.

Measurement

A horse was measured in "hands" from its feet to the top of its shoulders (the withers). One hand is equal to 4 in (10.16 cm). Black Beauty was 15.5 hands high – an average height for a carriage horse.

A "hand" is based on the average width of a man's hand.

Heavy shire horses were bred for hard work.

Fine hair, or "feather," on limbs

Chapter eight

A LONDON CAB HORSE

LONDON STREETS
The streets of London were noisy, dirty, and packed with crowds of horses pulling carriages, carts, trams, and buses.

I never knew such a merry family.

The cab stand
There were about 500 cab stands in London. Drivers, reluctant to leave their cabs in case they missed a fare, would often wait for hours in all weathers.

MY NEW MASTER'S NAME was Jeremiah Barker, but everyone called him Jerry. Polly, his wife, was as good a match as a man could have. The boy, Harry, was nearly twelve years old and little Dolly was eight. I never knew such a merry family. Nevertheless, my first week as a cab horse was trying. The noise, the hurry, the crowds of horses, carts, and carriages made me anxious.

But I soon found that I could trust my driver. Jerry never laid the whip on me; I knew when to go on by the way in which he took up the reins. In a short time my master and I understood each other as well as horse and man can.

Nothing was so near making Jerry angry as to find people wanting a cab horse to be driven hard to make up for their own idleness. However, he was not against putting on the steam, as he said, if he knew why.

I remember one morning, as we were on the stand waiting for a fare, a young man trod on a piece of orange peel and fell down with great force. Jerry was the first to run and lift him up. The man seemed much stunned.

"Can you take me to the South-Eastern Railway?" he asked. "This fall has made me late. It is of great importance that I should not miss the twelve o'clock train."

"I'll do my very best," said Jerry heartily, "if you think that you are well enough, sir," for the young man looked ill.

"I must go," he said earnestly. "Let us lose no time."

Jerry guided me, by the slightest touch of the rein, among carriages, buses, carts, vans, cabs, wagons, some going one way, some another, some going slowly, others wanting to pass, buses stopping short every few minutes to take up a passenger.

We whirled into the station. "We are in time!" said the young man. "Thank you, my friend, and your good horse. You have saved me more than money can ever pay for. Take this extra half-crown."

"No, sir, no, thank you all the same. It's quite pay enough for me to see how glad you are to catch the train."

Space on top for luggage

Driver's seat

Growler
Jerry probably drove a Clarence cab. These four-wheeled cabs were known as "growlers" because of the noise their iron wheels made on the roads.

"Thank you, my friend, and your good horse."

45

THE CRIMEAN WAR
The Crimean War (1853–56) was fought between Russia on the one side and Britain, France, Turkey, and Sardinia on the other. In the final charge by the British Light Brigade, hundreds of men and horses were killed.

Jerry's other cab horse was Captain. He was tall and white, and must have been quite splendid when young. His first owner was an officer of the cavalry going out to the Crimean War. Captain said he enjoyed training with the other cavalry horses.

"But what about the fighting?" said I.

"Well, I, with my noble master, went into many actions together without a wound. I don't think I feared for myself. My master's cheery voice, as he encouraged his men, made me feel as if he and I could not be killed. Until one dreadful day, I had never felt terror. That day I shall never forget."

Here old Captain paused for a while and drew a long breath.

"It was one autumn morning, and, as usual, the men mounted their horses, waiting for orders. As the light increased, we heard the firing of enemy guns. " 'We shall have a day of it today,' said my master quietly, as he smoothed my mane, 'but we'll do our duty as we have always done.' "

"I cannot tell all that happened, but I will tell of the last charge that we made together.

It was across a valley right in front of the enemy's cannon. We were well used to the roar of heavy guns and the rattle of musket fire, but never had I been under such a fire as we rode through on that day. From the right, from the left, and from the front, shot and shell poured in upon us. Many a horse fell, flinging his rider to the earth.

"Fearful as it was, no one turned back. Every moment the ranks thinned, but as our comrades fell, we closed in, galloping faster and faster as we neared the cannon, all clouded in white smoke.

"My dear master was cheering on his comrades with his arm raised high, when one of the balls, whizzing close to my head, struck him. I felt him stagger with the shock, then, sinking backward from the saddle, he fell to the earth. I wanted to keep my place by his side, and not leave him under that rush of horses' feet, but it was in vain. The greater number of men and creatures that went out that morning never came back."

Captain
Horses played a major part in warfare. White horses like Captain were ridden by officers and trumpeters.

Bayonet   Musket   Lead balls

Weapons
Foot soldiers used muskets. These were early versions of rifles that had the lead balls and powder rammed down the barrel. A bayonet could be attached for close fighting.

"One of the balls, whizzing close to my head, struck him."

One day, while our cab and many others were waiting outside one of the Parks, a shabby old cab drove up beside ours. The horse was an old, worn-out chestnut, with an ill-kept coat and bones that showed plainly through it. I had been eating some hay, and the wind rolled a little lock of it that way, and the poor creature put out her long, thin neck and picked it up, and then turned round and looked about for more. There was a hopeless look in the dull eye that I could not help noticing, and then, as I was thinking where I had seen that horse before, she looked full at me and said, "Black Beauty, is that you?"

It was Ginger! But how changed! The beautifully arched and glossy neck was now straight and lank. The face that was once so full of spirit and life was now full of suffering, and I could tell by the heaving of her sides and her frequent cough how bad her breath was.

Our drivers were standing together a little way off, so I sidled up to her a step or two, that we might have a little quiet talk. It was a sad tale that she had to tell.

After Earlshall, she was sold to a gentleman. For a little while she got on very well, but after a longer gallop than usual the old strain returned, and after being rested she was again sold. She changed hands several times, but always getting lower down.

"And so at last," said she, "I was bought by a man who keeps a number of cabs and horses and lets them out. You look well off, and I am glad of it, but I could not tell you what my life has been. The man who hires me now pays a deal of money to the owner every day, and so has to get it out of me, too; so it's all the week round and round, with never a Sunday rest."

It was Ginger! But how changed!

I said, "You used to stand up for yourself if you were ill-used."

"I did once," she said. "But it's no use. Men are strongest, and if they are cruel and have no feeling, there is nothing we can do but bear it, on and on until the end. I wish the end was come, I wish I was dead. I have seen dead horses, and I am sure they do not suffer pain; I wish I may drop down dead at my work."

I was very much troubled, and I put my nose up to hers, but I could say nothing to comfort her.

"You are the only friend I ever had," she said.

Just then, her driver came up, and with a tug at her mouth, backed her out of the line and drove off, leaving me very sad indeed.

A short time after this, a cart with a dead horse in it passed our cab stand. The head hung out of the cart-tail, the lifeless tongue was slowly dropping with blood; and the sunken eyes! It was a chestnut horse with a long thin neck and a white streak on the forehead. I believe it was Ginger. I hoped it was, for then her troubles would be over. Oh! If men were more merciful, they would shoot us before we came to such misery.

49

ELECTION TIME
Each party had their own color. The Conservatives wore blue and the Liberals wore orange.

Nosebag
While out working, horses were fed with a bag full of grain that was fitted over the head with a strap.

St. Thomas's
This was one of London's oldest hospitals, and was rebuilt on the south bank of the Thames River in 1871.

As we came into the yard one afternoon, Polly came out. "Jerry!" she called. "You've had one of the local candidates here asking about your vote, and he wants to hire your cab for the election."

"Well, Polly, you may say that my cab will be otherwise engaged. I should not like to have it pasted over with their great bills."

There was no lack of work for Jerry and me on election day in any case. After a very busy morning, we returned to the stand. Jerry put on my nosebag, which was filled with a good feed of crushed oats with bran. The streets were very full, and the cabs with the candidates' colors on them were dashing about through the crowd as if life and limb were of no consequence. Then a poor young woman carrying a child came along and asked Jerry the way to St. Thomas's Hospital. The child was crying. "He suffers a deal of pain," she said. "If I could get him to the hospital, he might get well."

"Why," said Jerry, "it is three miles away. I'll take you for nothing."

"Heaven bless you!" said the woman.

As Jerry went to open the door for her, two men, with colors in their hats, ran up, calling out "Cab!"

One of the men, pushing past the woman, sprang into the cab, followed by the other. "The cab is already engaged by this woman," said Jerry sternly. He refused to drive them anywhere. They got out, calling him all sorts of bad names. We soon reached the hospital and Jerry helped the young woman out.

"Thank you a thousand times," she said.

Just as we were leaving the hospital, a lady came down the steps. "Jeremiah Barker, is it you?" she said. "You are just the friend I want, for it is very difficult to get a cab today."

"I shall be proud to serve you, ma'am," said Jerry.

There was no lack of work for Jerry and me on election day.

We drove her to Paddington Station, and I learned that she, Mrs. Fowler, had been Polly's mistress. "How do you find the cab work suits you?" she asked.

One of the men, pushing past the woman, sprang into the cab, followed by the other.

"I'm getting on quite well, though it is all hours and all weathers, and that does try a man."

"Well, Barker," she said, "If ever you think you want to give up this cab work, let me know. There are many places where good drivers or good grooms are wanted."

Jerry thanked her and seemed much pleased, and turning out of the station, we at last reached home, and I, at least, was tired.

"How do you find the cab work suits you?" she asked.

51

Victorian Christmas
Christmas celebrations as we know them, with trees, cards, and crackers, began in the nineteenth century.

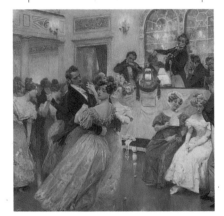

London society
Fashionable balls were held regularly among rich people, but especially at Christmas and New Year.

Card games
Some people were known as the "at homes," because they stayed in playing cards and other games. Cards and dancing were seen as sinful by strict Christians.

Christmas and the New Year are merry times for some people, but for cabmen and cabmen's horses it is no holiday. There are so many parties and balls that the work is hard and often late. We had a great deal of work in the Christmas week, and Jerry's cough was bad.

On the evening of the New Year, we took two gentlemen to a house in one of the West End squares. We set them down at nine o'clock and were told to come again at eleven.

"But," said one of them, "as it is a card party, you may have to wait a few minutes, but don't be late."

As the clock struck eleven, we were at the door, for Jerry was always punctual. The clock chimed the quarters – one, two, three, and then struck twelve, but the door did not open. The wind had been very changeable, with squalls of rain during the day, but now it came on sharp, driving sleet. It was very cold, and there was no shelter. At half-past-twelve, Jerry rang the bell and asked if he would be wanted that night.

"Oh, yes," said the butler. "The game will soon be over."

By then Jerry's voice was so hoarse, I could hardly hear him.

At a quarter past one, the door opened, and the two gentlemen came out. They got into the cab and told Jerry where to drive. My legs were numb with cold, and I thought I should stumble. When the men got out they never said they were sorry to have kept us waiting so long, but were angry at the charge for two hours and a quarter waiting time.

At last we got home. Jerry could hardly speak, and his cough was dreadful.

It was late the next morning before anyone came into the stable, and then it was only Harry. He neither whistled nor sang while he fed us and swept out the stalls. At noon, he came again. This time little Dolly came with him. She was crying, and I gathered from what they said that Jerry was dangerously ill.

He grew better steadily, but the doctor said that Jerry must never go back to the cab work again if he wished to be an old man.

One afternoon, Dolly came dancing into the stable.

"Mother has got a letter from Mrs. Fowler," she told Harry. "She says we are all to go and live near her. Her coachman is going away in the spring and then she will want Father in his place!"

It was quickly settled that as soon as Jerry was well, they should move to the country, and that the cab and horses should be sold.

This was heavy news for me, for I was not young now, and three years of cab work will tell on one's strength. I felt I was not the horse that I had once been.

Hard times
A cabdriver's life was a hard one. They were poorly paid and worked long hours. Some passengers took them for granted, expecting them to wait for hours in the freezing cold.

The clock struck twelve, but the door did not open.

Black Beauty's London

Hansom cab

When Black Beauty arrived in London, he found the noise and the bustle overwhelming. The roads were packed with people, and with horses pulling every type of vehicle – from light carriages and cabs to heavy wagons, omnibuses, and trams.

Omnibus

There were about 800 horse-drawn omnibuses in London at this time. The work was very hard for the horses because the buses were so heavy to pull. A two-horse bus changed horses up to six times a day.

The Cabs of London Town

Cabs were an essential means of transportation. There were about four times more cabs than omnibuses or trams.

The hansom and the growler were the two main types of cabs.

Driver's seat

Hansom

Two-wheeled hansom cabs were faster and more stylish than growlers. Their drivers tended to be wealthier and their horses in better condition.

The growler

The four-wheeled growler was the poor relation of the hansom, but was in some ways more practical. It was roomier inside, with plenty of space for luggage, and was often used to take passengers to and from railroad stations.

Dark horse

Cab horses were usually brown or chestnut. Gray was less popular, since it showed the dirt. The horses were worked hard for two or three years, and were then often sold.

Cab shelter

Some cab stands had shelters that provided drivers with food, drink, and warmth. They were cramped inside, because they could not take up more space than that used by a horse and cab.

Cost of a cab

The cabdriver could pay up to 18 shillings a day (about $1.80) to hire a cab and two horses, and yet could only charge a cab fare of 6 d (about 5 cents) a mile (1.6 km).

Rush hour

Thousands of people crossed London Bridge every day on their way to and from work. Many people preferred to walk rather than face being held up on the congested roads.

The mounted police were usually used in the less crowded outskirts of London, but starting in 1870 they also helped with crowd control in the center of the city.

Trams

There were about 350 tram cars in London. Trams were easier to pull than buses – the smooth movement of the steel wheels on rails meant horses could pull nearly twice as many passengers.

CAB	TRAM	OMNIBUS
Cabs were pulled by one horse. They carried up to six people and traveled at up to 15 mph (24 km/h).	Trams were pulled by two horses. They carried up to 48 people and traveled at 7 mph (11 km/h).	Omnibuses were pulled by 2–3 horses. They carried up to 28 people and traveled at 8 mph (13 km/h).

Horse trams were in general use up until the end of the 19th century.

The London cabby

The life of a London cabdriver was a hard one. They worked long hours – sometimes up to 16 hours a day. Jerry owned his own cab and horses, but many drivers had to rent them.

Roads were cobbled or paved with stone slabs.

Most people drove on the left-hand side of the road, but there were no strict rules.

Sunday rest

Jerry always insisted that he should rest with his family on Sunday, despite pressure to work. There were no paid holidays for cabbies.

Ale house

When the weather was bad, cabmen often visited the local tavern for a drink. Alcoholism was at an all-time high in the 1870s, and was one major cause of road accidents.

Accidents

Collisions were common on the busy London streets. There were no driving tests, and driving skills varied greatly. Driving around corners too quickly was a particular hazard, often resulting in a horse being injured by a carriage shaft running into its chest.

Corn dealer and baker
This trade involved buying and selling all types of grain, as well as baking and selling bread.

Two-wheeled carts could carry about half a ton of produce.

Horse and cart
Horses were used by farmers and tradespeople. Carters were employed to drive the vehicles.

A kind driver would use a whip to tap the horse lightly rather than hurt it.

Cart whip

Chapter nine

HARD TIMES

I WAS SOLD TO A CORN DEALER AND BAKER whom Jerry knew, and with him he thought I should have good food and fair work. In the first he was quite right, but there was a foreman who, when I had a full load, would order something else to be taken on.

One day, I was loaded more than usual and part of the road was a steep uphill. I used all my strength, but I could not get on, and was obliged continually to stop. This did not please my carter, Jakes, and he laid his whip on badly.

"Get on, you lazy fellow," he said, "or I'll make you."

The pain of that great cart whip was sharp, but my mind was hurt quite as much as my poor sides. To be punished and abused when I was doing my very best was so hard it took the heart out of me. He was flogging me cruelly, when a lady stepped quickly up to him.

"Pray do not whip your good horse any more," she said in a sweet, earnest voice. "The road is very steep, and he is doing his best."

"If doing his best won't get this load up, he must do something more than his best," said Jakes.

"But is it not a very heavy load?" she said.

"Yes, too heavy," he said, "but that's not my fault. I must get on with it as well as I can."

He was raising the whip again when the lady said, "You do not give him a fair chance. He cannot use all his power with his head held back as it is with that bearing rein. If you would take it off, I am sure he would do better. Do try it," she said persuasively. "I should be very glad if you would."

Jakes gave a short laugh. "Anything to please a lady."

The rein was taken off, and in a moment I put my head down to my very knees. What a comfort it was! Then I tossed it up and down several times to get the aching stiffness out of my neck.

"Poor fellow! That is what you wanted," said she, patting and stroking me with her gentle hand. "And now if you will speak kindly to him and lead him on, I believe he will be able to do better."

"Poor fellow! That is what you wanted," said she, stroking me with her gentle hand.

Jakes took the rein. "Come on, Blackie."

I put down my head and threw my whole weight against the collar. I spared no strength. The load moved on, and I pulled it steadily up the hill, and then stopped to take breath.

"You see he was quite willing when you gave him the chance," said the lady. "You won't put that rein on again, will you?"

"Well, ma'am, I can't deny that having his head has helped him up the hill. But if he went without a bearing rein I should be the laughing stock of all the carters. It is the fashion you see."

"Is it not better," she said, "to lead a good fashion, than to follow a bad one? Besides, we have no right to distress any of God's creatures without a very good reason. They cannot tell us how they feel, but they do not suffer less because they have no words."

Horse's collar

The collar is the part of the harness that fits around the horse's neck and is attached to the load with chains.

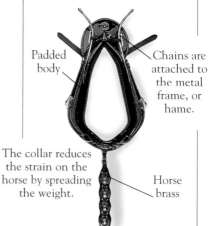

Padded body

Chains are attached to the metal frame, or hame.

The collar reduces the strain on the horse by spreading the weight.

Horse brass

Skinner had a low set of cabs and a low set of drivers.

Heavy load
Cabs were allowed up to six passengers, but there was no limit to the amount of luggage they could carry.

Ludgate Hill
This street in the city of London leads from Fleet Street and Ludgate Circus up to St. Paul's Cathedral.

I shall never forget my next master. He had black eyes and a hooked nose, and his voice was as harsh as the grinding of cart wheels over gravel stones. His name was Nicholas Skinner.

Skinner had a low set of cabs and a low set of drivers. He was hard on the men, and the men were hard on the horses. We had no Sunday rest, and it was in the heat of summer. My driver was just as hard as my master. He had a cruel whip, and would even whip me under the belly, and flip the lash out at my head. My life was now so wretched that I wished I might, like Ginger, drop down dead and be out of my misery. One day my wish nearly came to pass.

We had to take a fare at the railway. There was a party of four: a noisy, blustering man with a lady, a little boy, and a young girl, and a great deal of luggage. The young girl came and looked at me.

"Papa," she said, "I am sure this poor horse cannot take us and all our luggage so far. Do look at him."

The porter suggested to the gentleman, as there was so much luggage, whether he would not take a second cab.

"Papa, do take a second cab," said the young girl. "I am sure it is very cruel."

"Get in, Grace, and don't make all this fuss," said the father.

My gentle friend had to obey, and box after box was loaded on. At last all was ready. I got along fairly till we came to Ludgate Hill, but there the heavy load and my own exhaustion were too much. I was struggling to keep on, goaded by constant chucks of the rein and use of the whip, when, in a single moment my feet slipped from under me and I fell heavily to the ground. The force with which I fell seemed to beat all the breath out of my body. I lay perfectly still; I had no power to move, and I thought now I was going to die.

I heard a sort of confusion around me, and thought I heard that sweet, pitiful voice say, "That poor horse! It is our fault."

Someone loosened my bridle and collar. Then I could hear the policeman giving orders, but I did not even open my eyes. I cannot tell how long I lay there, but after several attempts, I managed to stagger to my feet, and a kind man led me to some stables which were close by. Some warm gruel was brought to me, which I drank thankfully. In the evening, I was led back to Skinner's stables.

In the morning, Skinner came with a farrier who examined me very closely and said: "This is a case of overwork more than disease. There is not an ounce of strength left in him."

"Then he must go to the dogs," said Skinner. "I have no meadows to nurse sick horses in. That sort of thing doesn't suit my business."

"There is a sale of horses coming off in about ten days," said the farrier. "If you rest him and feed him, he may pick up, and you may get more than his skin is worth, at any rate."

Upon this advice, Skinner gave orders that I should be well fed and cared for. Ten days of perfect rest and plenty of good food, and I began to think, after all, it might be better to live than go to the dogs, so I held up my head, and hoped for the best.

At this sale, I noticed a gentleman farmer with a young boy.

"Poor old fellow! Grandpapa, could you not buy him and make him young again?"

I arched my poor thin neck, raised my tail a little, and threw out my legs as well as I could, for they were very stiff.

"'Tis a speculation," said the old gentleman, shaking his head, but at the same time slowly drawing out his purse. The boy could hardly control his delight as I was gently ridden home by a servant of my new master's.

My feet slipped from under me and I fell heavily to the ground.

On the beat
The police were responsible for keeping the roads clear of traffic jams. People who drove too fast and endangered the lives of others were fined.

Horse care
With regular exercise and good food and care, horses should stay healthy well into old age.

Chapter ten

MY LAST HOME

M R. THOROUGHGOOD, for that was the name of my benefactor, gave orders that I should have hay and oats every night and morning, and the run of the meadow during the day, and "You, Willie," he said to his grandson, "must oversee him."

The boy was proud of his charge, and undertook it in all seriousness. The perfect rest, the good food, the soft turf, and gentle exercise soon began to tell on my condition and my spirits.

Three ladies came out and looked at me.

"He's growing young, Willie," said Mr. Thoroughgood. "We must now be looking for a quiet, genteel place for him, where he will be valued."

One day during the summer, Willie got into the chaise with his grandfather. At the distance of a mile or two from the village, we came to a pretty house. Three ladies came out and looked at me. The youngest lady – that was Miss Ellen – took to me very much. Miss Lavinia said that she should always be nervous riding behind a horse that had once been down, as I might come down again.

"Many first-rate horses have had their knees broken through the carelessness of their drivers, " said Mr. Thoroughgood. "From what I see of this horse, I should say that is his case. If he is not as safe as any horse you ever drove, send him back."

The next day, when my new groom was cleaning my face, he said, "That is just like the star that Black Beauty had. I wonder where he is now." A little further on he came to the place in my neck where I was bled, and where a little knot was left in the skin.

"White star in the forehead, one white foot, this little knot just in

Star

Star and stripe

Freckled stripe

Markings
The white markings on a horse's face have special names, like Black Beauty's "star" – a mark between or above the eyes.

that place – as I am alive, it must be Black Beauty! Why, Beauty, do you know me? Little Joe Green that almost killed you?"

And he began patting me as if he was quite overjoyed. I could not say that I recognized him, for now he was a fine-grown young fellow, with black whiskers and a man's voice.

"I wonder who the rascal was that broke your knees, my old Beauty! Well, it won't be my fault if you haven't good times of it now. I wish John Manly was here to see you."

I soon found that Miss Ellen was a good drive. I heard Joe telling her that he was sure I was Squire Gordon's old Black Beauty. She said, "I shall write to Mrs. Gordon, and tell her that her favorite horse has come to us!"

I have now lived in this happy place a whole year. Joe is the best and kindest of grooms. My ladies have promised

"Why, Beauty, do you know me?"

My troubles are over and I am at home.

that I shall never be sold, and so I have nothing to fear. My troubles are over, and I am at home. Often, before I am quite awake, I fancy I am still in the orchard at Birtwick, standing with my old friends under the apple trees.

ANNA SEWELL'S HORSES

Anna Sewell was born into a world where horses were the main means of transportion. Since the development of the railroad, horses were used less for long distances, but were needed all the more for short journeys. Horses were a necessity – they were working animals, not pets – and they were often treated harshly. It was this mistreatment that Anna Sewell protested against in her novel.

ANNA SEWELL

Born in Great Yarmouth, Anna Sewell (1820–78) was only a baby when the family moved to London. Her parents were Quakers, and Sewell had a strict religious upbringing. She loved horses from an early age. Plagued by poor health, she wrote Black Beauty *during the last seven years of her life.*

Anna Sewell

Who it was written for

In her novel, Anna Sewell shows a detailed knowledge of horses, the work they did, and the people they worked with. The novel was written for these people – the grooms, stablehands, and drivers – rather than for children.

Horse and groom

Campaign against cruelty

Anna Sewell was not alone in her campaign. There was a growing concern for animal welfare in the 1870s that was supported by the RSPCA (Royal Society for the Prevention of Cruelty to Animals). Many books and articles were written speaking out against mistreatment of the working horse and particularly the use of the bearing rein.

A wish fulfilled

At Anna Sewell's funeral, a team of horses with bearing reins attached arrived to collect the coffin, and the author's mother demanded they be removed. By the beginning of the 1900s, the bearing rein was no longer in general use, although undertakers continued to use it on their horses until 1914.

Black funeral horses, draped i black velvet

Early editions

The first edition was published in 1877 and was an immediate success. In 1890 it appeared in the US, where a million copies were sold within the first two years. Hundreds of editions have been published since then, and the book has never been out of print.

Illustration of Lady Anne, from the 1894 edition

Illustrations by Cecil Aldin, from the 1912 edition

Best-seller

Today, *Black Beauty*'s popularity continues. Movie and television adaptations have been made, and the novel itself remains a firm favorite with many children and adults.

The horses tha starred in the fil *Black Beauty*, ma in 1994

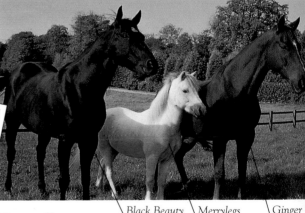

Black Beauty \ Merrylegs \ Ginger

On a busy London street, a horse's head is pulled back by a tightened bearing rein.

RSPCA

Early British editions of Black Beauty were recommended by the RSPCA, which was founded in 1824. In 1914, the RSPCA enforced the removal of the bearing rein on all horse-drawn vehicles, and Anna Sewell's dearest wish was realized.

Horse with docked tail

Short tail

Anna Sewell spoke out against the fashionable practice of docking tails, in which the tail bone was cut off to stop the tail hairs from growing too long.

Bearing rein

The tighter the bearing rein, the higher the horse's head was held. It meant the horse wore two bits, one for the bearing rein, one for the bridle. Some bits were sharp and could cut the horse's mouth. Today, bits are designed so they do not hurt the horse.

Modern bit with smooth steel bar

Blind eye

Anna Sewell thought blinkers were unnecessary, but they are still used today. They prevent the horse from seeing sideways.

Blinkers

A hard life

People often mistreated their horses not intentionally, but through ignorance, or because they were badly off themselves. Many horses were overworked because their owners, especially cabdrivers, were poorly paid and had to work long hours.

HORSES IN THE 20TH CENTURY

Horseless power

It was the arrival of the automobile in the 1880s that marked the beginning of the end of the horse and carriage. Cars were often built and painted by traditional coach makers.

This early car had wooden wheels and bodywork, just like a horse-drawn carriage.

Horses today

In general, horses today are not expected to work in the way Black Beauty, and many like him, once did.

Horses are still used in some countries for farming.

Horses are often used for sports and recreation, with many children learning to ride for fun.

Acknowledgments

Picture Credits
The publisher would like to thank the following for their kind permission to reproduce their photographs:

t=top, b=bottom, a=above,
c=center, l=left, r=right.

Bridgeman Art Library, London: Aberdeen Art Gallery and Museum 32clb; Christie's, London 9trb; City of York Art Gallery, York 43tc; Gavin Graham Gallery, London 10tl; Harrowgate Museums and Art Gallery 43cl; Historisches Museum der Stadt, Vienna 52cl; London Library, London 26tl; Josef Mensing Gallery, Hamm-Rhynern 44bl; Private Collection 29tr, 52tl, 63trb; Phillips the Auctioneers 9tr; Sheffield Art Galleries 28tl; The Maas Gallery, London 23br; Walker Art Gallery, Liverpool 38cl; Weston Park, Shropshire 39cl.
Edifice: Philippa Lewis 18tl.
Mary Evans Picture Library: Back Flap tl, 18cl, 27tr, 32cl, 32bc, 35tr, 36bl, 44tl, 50tl, 53tr, 54cr, 54/55, 55cr, 55cb, 55br, 56tl, 62tlb, 62c, 62clb, 62bca, 62bc, 63cl.
Robert Harding Picture Library: 52bl.
Hulton Getty Picture Collection: 50bl, 54bl, 58bl, 59tr.
Kit Houghton: 35cr, 35br.
Kobal Collection: 63br.

Bob Langrish: 1c, 7(whole page), 60tr.
London Transport Museum: 54tr, 55tl.
Mansell Collection: 54tl, 63tl.
John Mauger: 36tl.
National Trust Photographic Library: 33br.
The Royal Mint, Llantrisant: 39tl, 43bc.
RSPCA Photo Library: 63tr.

The following horses and their owners: 19tr Avelignese – Noaner, Instituto Incremento Ippico Di Crema, Italy; 19cr Saddlebred – Kinda Kostly, Kentucky Horse Park, USA; 30cl Connemara – Garryhack Tooreen, Mrs Beckett, Shipton Connemara Pony Stud, UK; 39tr Frederiksborg – Zarif Langløkkegard, Harry Nielsen; 39bl Percheron – Tango, Haras National de Saint Lô, France; 42bl Westphalian – Sian Thomas BHSI, Snowdonia Equestrian Centre, UK; 43crb Thoroughbred – Lyphento, Conkwell Grange Stud, Avon; 43br Shire – Duke, Jim Lockwood, Courage Shire Horse Centre, Buckinghamshire.

Additional photography: Andy Crawford and Gary Ombler at the DK Photographic Studio; Norman Hollands; Sam Scott-Hunter; Richard Leaney; Alex Wilson; Victoria Hall.

Additional illustrations: David Ashby, Roger Hutchins, Stephen Gjaypay, Sallie Alane Reason, Rodney Shackell.

DK would particularly like to thank the following people:

Angels & Bermans, London; Bridgeman Art Library; ET Archive; Mary Evans Picture Library; Victoria Hall for research assistance; Joanna Hartley; Colin Henderson, The Royal Mews, Buckingham Palace; John Mauger, carriage consultant; Rebecca at Swaine Adeney Brigg, London; Risky Business, London; The London Fire Brigade Museum; London Transport Museum; Stonar School, Wiltshire; Gwen and Jeff Leonard; and Alexandra Warwick for her invaluable advice and help with costume and accessories; Marion Dent for proofreading.

Models: Jon Collins, Ross Maceacharn, Roy Still, Alexandra Warwick, and Glyn Morgan.